You Choose Stories: Superman
is published by Stone Arch Books,
A Capstone Imprint
1710 Roe Crest Drive
North Mankato, Minnesota 56003
www.mycapstone.com

STAR39713

Cataloging-in-Publication Data is available
on the Library of Congress website.
ISBN: 978-1-4965-5824-4 (library binding)
ISBN: 978-1-4965-5829-9 (paperback)
ISBN: 978-1-4965-5835-0 (eBook)

Summary: The city of Metropolis is holding a special
celebration to honor Superman. But when Bizarro arrives,
disaster soon follows. He wants to be like his hero,
Superman. But Bizarro ends up causing major problems
across the city instead. Only you can help Superman stop
Bizarro before he completely wrecks Metropolis!

Printed in the United States of America.
010830S18

← YOU CHOOSE →

SUPERMAN™

SUPERMAN DAY
DISASTER

Superman created by
Jerry Siegel and Joe Shuster
by special arrangement with the Jerry Siegel Family

written by
Steve Korté

illustrated by
Dario Brizuela

STONE ARCH BOOKS
a capstone imprint

Bizarro wants to be just like his hero,
Superman. But he unwittingly causes major
destruction and chaos across Metropolis. Only
YOU can help stop him. With your help, the
Man of Steel can put a stop to Bizarro's path
of destruction in *Superman Day Disaster*!

Follow the directions at the bottom of
each page. The choices YOU make will change
the outcome of the story. After you finish one
path, go back and read the others for more
Superman adventures!

BUZZZ! BUZZZ! BUZZZ!

On a hot summer morning in Metropolis, Clark Kent slowly opens one eye to glare at the beeping alarm clock next to his bed. With a groan, he reaches out his hand and pushes a button on top of the clock to silence it.

"Just a few more minutes of sleep," Clark mutters to himself, as he buries his head beneath his pillow.

CHIRP! CHIRP! CHIRP!

Two minutes later, the birds outside Clark's apartment window start singing to each other.

Clark opens his eyes and sighs. Bright sunlight is shining through the bedroom window directly onto his bed. Reluctantly, he realizes that it's time to get up and climbs out of bed.

"Today's the big day," Clark says to himself. "I'd better get ready quickly."

Turn the page.

Doing things quickly is no problem for Clark Kent. He is secretly Superman — the world's most powerful hero.

With a blast of super-speed, Clark zips around his apartment in a flash. He brushes his teeth, combs his hair, gets dressed, and gobbles down his breakfast in less than ten seconds.

A few minutes later, Clark is walking along the sidewalk on this hot July morning. He's headed to the offices of the *Daily Planet* newspaper, where he works as a reporter.

Today is Superman Day in Metropolis. Some of the city's most important citizens will be gathered in front of the Daily Planet Building to honor Superman, the Man of Steel!

Clark chuckles quietly and says to himself, "Today should be interesting. I get to write a story about Superman Day. But as Superman, I *also* get to be the guest of honor!"

A little while later, Clark arrives in downtown Metropolis. Although it's still early in the morning, the temperature is rapidly rising.

The hot weather hasn't kept the crowds away, however. The sidewalks are jammed with men and women and children, all hoping to get a glimpse of their beloved hero Superman.

A parade is moving down the street. The sound of a marching band fills the air. In the middle of the street is a large red and blue float with a statue of Superman on top of it.

Turn the page.

"Clark! Over here!" calls out a woman's voice.

Clark looks up and smiles at Lois Lane, his friend and one of the best reporters at the *Daily Planet*. She's standing on a platform in front of the building with a dozen other people.

"You're late, Clark," says Lois with a frown. "Superman is due here any minute!"

Clark steps closer to the platform and stands next to a young man with bright red hair who is holding a camera. It's Clark's good friend Jimmy Olsen, who is a photographer for the *Daily Planet*.

Jimmy turns to Clark and says, "Sure is a hot one today, Mister Kent."

Clark nods in agreement and then takes a few steps back, moving away from Jimmy.

"You're right, Jimmy, it's awfully hot today. I'll be back in a minute. I left something important in my office," Clark replies, edging his way through the crowd toward the building's entrance.

"You'd better hurry, Mister Kent," says Jimmy. "The parade has already started. You don't want to miss seeing Superman!"

Clark smiles at Jimmy and says, "Oh, I don't think I need to worry about that."

Clark enters the building and quickly finds an empty office.

With a few lightning-fast moves, Clark removes his shirt and tie to reveal his Superman uniform.

Turn the page.

WHOOOOOOOSH!

"Hooray!" the people cheer as Superman zooms through the air. The Man of Steel lands on the platform in front of the Daily Planet Building. He waves to the happy crowd.

"Thank you for coming out to see me on this hot day," Superman calls out to the people.

WHOOOOOOOSH!

Suddenly, another sound is heard high above the crowd.

"Look! Up in the sky!" someone yells. "Is that *another* Superman?"

All eyes look up in the air. The people gasp as another figure flies above the Daily Planet Building. He's wearing a uniform similar to Superman's with a bright red cape. But he has chalky white skin and crooked teeth.

It's the strange creature Bizarro!

"Hello, Metropolis people!" Bizarro yells, as a crooked smile fills his face. "Me not want to miss the fun!"

But Bizarro isn't watching where he's flying.

BLAM!

He slams against the wall of a nearby building and then flies into a flagpole.

"Oops!" says Bizarro. His cape is now wrapped tightly around the flagpole. He pulls on his cape and tries to untangle it. With a mighty tug, he yanks the cape free. But the flagpole snaps, and it falls to the ground.

"It not easy being hero," Bizarro mutters.

Superman frowns as he watches the creature hover high above the platform. Bizarro was created as a clone of Superman, but Bizarro's superpowers are opposite to the Man of Steel's. He has freeze-vision instead of heat-vision. And unlike Superman's freezing cold breath, Bizarro shoots red-hot flames out of his mouth.

Turn the page.

Lois Lane turns to Superman and asks, "Is this creature dangerous?"

"He's not evil," Superman replies. "But Bizarro does cause a lot of trouble when he tries to be like me."

Perry White, the editor of the *Daily Planet*, overhears their conversation.

"How does that cause trouble?" asks Perry.

Superman sighs and says, "Unfortunately, Bizarro does things backward. He always gets everything wrong when he tries to be a hero."

"Me here to be with best friend Superman!" Bizarro calls out, as he floats closer to the Man of Steel.

"This is going to be a problem," says Superman with a sigh.

If Bizarro decides to land next to Superman, turn to page 16.

If Superman chooses to confront Bizarro in the air, turn to page 18.

If Bizarro flies closer to the parade, turn to page 20.

CRASH!

"Me want to join party!" announces Bizarro as he tumbles onto the platform, falling over with a loud thud.

Bizarro stands up and pushes his way to the front of the platform. He shoves the police chief and the mayor of Metropolis out of the way to move closer to the Man of Steel.

Bizarro stretches a hand out toward Superman. In his hand is a small metal box.

"Me have special gift for Superman!" Bizarro says proudly.

The mayor then pushes his way back to the front of the platform. "We're presenting Superman with the key to the city at the *end* of the parade!" he exclaims. "You can give him your gift then."

Bizarro shakes his head with annoyance and says, "No, this gift better than stupid key. This something that Superman loves!"

"Uh-oh," says Superman to himself. "If this is something Bizarro thinks I'll love, then it's probably something awful!"

Superman quickly focuses his X-ray vision on the box, trying to look inside. But the box is made out of lead. Lead is the one substance that Superman can't see through.

If Bizarro decides to open the box, turn to page 22.
If Bizarro chooses not to open the box, turn to page 29.

Bizarro moves closer to the platform in front of the Daily Planet Building. Many in the crowd are fearful of the creature.

Lois Lane turns to Superman and asks, "What are you going to do?"

"I'm going to have a little talk with Bizarro," says Superman.

ZOOOOOM!

Superman launches himself into the air and flies close to Bizarro.

The Man of Steel faces the creature and says sternly, "Bizarro, you're not supposed to be here. The last time we met . . ."

"Me know, me know," Bizarro says. "Me agreed not to come back. But me heard about Superman Day party. And me had to come because Bizarro am just like Superman!"

Superman frowns and reaches out to grab Bizarro's wrist.

"You can't stay here," says the Man of Steel.

"Me know," Bizarro says sadly.

"You do?" Superman asks with surprise. It's usually not this easy to convince Bizarro to leave.

"With Superman busy at party, me no can stay here with you," the creature replies. "There am no one else to protect city. Bizarro am going to be hero of Metropolis today. Me am ready!"

An alarmed look comes over Superman's face.

"No, Bizarro," he says. "That's not what . . ."

"No time to talk," Bizarro says. "Bizarro have busy day ahead. Me first say goodbye to Superman's friends."

"Wait, Bizarro," says Superman.

Bizarro suddenly dives down, but he's moving too fast and crashes into the platform. The impact shatters two of the wooden support beams below the platform. The entire platform begins to sway dangerously to one side.

Superman quickly flies down to repair the platform. As he does so, Bizarro flies away.

If Bizarro heads for downtown Metropolis, turn to page 25.
If Bizarro flies toward the river, turn to page 31.

Bizarro hovers above the platform in front of the Daily Planet Building. He is watching the parade as it moves down the street. He holds a small metal box in one hand. Suddenly a loud sound fills the air.

HOOONNNK! HOOONNNK!

A bright red fire truck in the parade is blowing its loud horn with an ear-shattering sound.

Bizarro smiles with delight and claps his hands together, causing the metal box to tumble from his hand. The box falls unnoticed onto the platform. Bizarro flies over to the fire truck and lands on top of it.

"Me ride big red truck in parade for Superman!" Bizarro announces.

HOOOONNNK!

Bizarro claps his hands again and jumps through the air to land on the platform next to Superman.

"Me have fun ride on red truck," Bizarro says, standing up.

The people on the street stare at Bizarro in astonishment. Superman reaches out to grab Bizarro, but the creature pulls away.

"Me happy to be here at Superman party," he announces loudly to the crowd.

The parade has stopped moving, and the crowd stays silent. They are waiting to see what Superman is going to do.

Bizarro turns to Superman and whispers, "No one talking or moving. Me think it too hot today. Bizarro will help."

If Bizarro decides to join the parade, turn to page 27.
If Bizarro chooses to stay on the platform, turn to page 33.

Bizarro opens the lid of the box. Inside the box is a small green rock. It's green Kryptonite, the one substance that can weaken or even kill Superman!

The Man of Steel reaches forward to try to close the box. But he's already weakened by the Kryptonite and can only knock the box out of Bizarro's hand. When the box hits the floor, the Kryptonite tumbles out and rolls unnoticed into a crack.

The Kryptonite is still too close to Superman, causing him to lose his powers. The Man of Steel falls facedown onto the platform.

"Superman love my gift so much he faints!" Bizarro says proudly.

"What have you done?!" Lois Lane shouts at Bizarro.

Bizarro turns to Lois and smiles at her.

"You very pretty," he says bashfully. "Me think you would like to marry Bizarro."

"Marry you?" Lois says with astonishment.

"Okay, me accept," Bizarro says happily, as he gets down on one knee.

He reaches out to grasp Lois' hand and says, "Me soon take you to home of your dreams."

BZZZZZ! BZZZZZ!

Perry White's cellphone is buzzing.

Perry listens for a moment and then turns to the police chief.

"There's a break-in at the Metropolis Savings and Loan Bank," says Perry.

Bizarro looks troubled by this news.

"Me not know what to do," the creature says. "Do me go to bank and be hero? Or do me take Lois Lane to new home?"

If Bizarro flies to the bank, turn to page 36.
If Bizarro carries Lois away, turn to page 52.

"Me going to have big adventures today," boasts Bizarro as he soars over the city. "Me show Superman that me can be *big* hero!"

Soon Bizarro flies over a large construction zone. A big building is in the process of being built. Several dozen tall beams are anchored in the ground. Because of the Superman Day celebration, there are no workers there.

Bizarro hovers over the construction site and says, "Me hungry. Maybe me find snack here."

The creature swoops down to the ground and finds an open cardboard box filled with nails.

CRUNCH! CRUNCH! CRUNCH!

"Yum!" he says, as he gobbles down a handful of sharp nails. "Bizarro find tasty snack filled with healthy iron!"

Turn the page.

A few seconds later, Bizarro's stomach begins to rumble.

"Uh-oh!" he says. "Snack no agree with Bizarro!"

BUUUURRRP!

Bizarro burps, causing a red-hot blast of fire to shoot out of his mouth.

The flames instantly melt several of the beams anchored to the ground. Soon a roaring fire is spreading through the entire construction site.

WHOOOSH!

Superman zooms into view. He has arrived to put out the fire.

"Move out of the way, Bizarro!" he calls out. "I'm going to use my freeze-breath to put out the flames."

The creature looks up at Superman and says happily, "Me help Superman!"

"No," insists the Man of Steel. "I don't need your help!

If Bizarro tries to help Superman anyway, turn to page 38.
If Bizarro decides to fly away, turn to page 56.

Bizarro jumps off the platform and lands in the middle of the parade. He walks over to the sidewalk and smiles at a woman who is holding a tiny brown dachshund dog in her hands. The woman backs away from Bizarro in fright.

"Me Bizarro," he says. "Me glad to meet woman and her hot dog."

Suddenly, Bizarro starts to laugh hysterically.

"Ha, ha! Me make funny joke!" he says, gasping for air between his laughs. "It hot today. And dog in your hands look like hot dog!"

Bizarro leans down to pet the dachshund. The dog snarls and shows its teeth.

CHOMP!

The dog bites Bizarro's chalky white hand.

Bizarro is unharmed and smiles at the dog.

"Nice doggy," he says. "Dog shows he like Bizarro. Me like hot dog too!"

Turn the page.

Superman flies over to Bizarro.

"I appreciate you offering to help, Bizarro," says Superman. "But there's nothing we can do about the hot weather."

Bizarro looks around at the people. Many are sweating from the heat. Bizarro then stares up at the blazing hot sun.

"Superman right," he says sadly. "No can change sun."

The Man of Steel sighs with relief. Now if he can convince Bizarro to leave Metropolis, the Superman Day celebration can continue.

Bizarro suddenly snaps his fingers and smiles at Superman.

"Me know!" Bizarro announces. "Bizarro know how to cool off people."

"No, Bizarro, don't . . ." says Superman.

Bizarro soars into the air and says, "Bizarro have big decision. Do me freeze street or do me open fire hydrants?"

If Bizarro freezes the street, turn to page 40.
If Bizarro breaks open the fire hydrants, turn to page 59.

Superman steps forward and takes the box from Bizarro's hands.

Whatever is in this lead box, thinks Superman, *it's something that I'm not going to like.*

"You open present now?" asks Bizarro eagerly.

"Uh, no," replies Superman, as he places the box down onto the platform.

Superman turns to Bizarro and says, "I think I should save it for after our trip."

"Trip?" says Bizarro with surprise. "You and me take trip together? Maybe you and me be heroes together?"

"Well, not exactly . . ." Superman says, trying not to deceive Bizarro.

Superman clasps Bizarro's hand and starts to soar above the platform. The creature rises in the air alongside the Man of Steel.

Turn the page.

Bizarro tugs his hand away from Superman. The creature plummets back to the floor of the wooden platform.

BLAM!

Bizarro stands on the platform and crosses his arms. A frown fills his face as he starts to pout.

"You no want Bizarro to be heroes with you, and you no want me at party," he says sadly. He reaches down and picks up the lead box.

"You not even want Bizarro's present," he says, as he starts to cry.

Superman returns to the platform and floats a few feet above Bizarro.

"Bizarro," Superman says sternly. "You need to come with me."

The creature sniffs back a tear and looks up at Superman.

"Well . . ." Bizarro begins.

If Bizarro agrees to leave with Superman, turn to page 70.
If Bizarro refuses to leave with Superman, turn to page 86.

"Me going to be big hero," says Bizarro as he zooms into the air. "Me show Superman that me can help!"

Soon, Bizarro flies high above the West River near downtown Metropolis.

"Look at pretty boats in water," Bizarro says, soaring closer to the river. A few sailboats are bobbing gently in the water, barely moving due to the lack of wind.

"Maybe me help boats move faster with super-breath," Bizarro says.

The creature takes a deep breath. But before he can blast the boats with his dangerous flame-breath, a loud sound fills the air.

WOOOOOOT!

It's the horn of a large ship traveling down the river toward a drawbridge. The captain of the ship is blowing the horn to alert the engineer on the bridge. It's time to raise the drawbridge so the ship can pass under it.

Turn the page.

Bizarro soars high above the drawbridge. He looks puzzled. He doesn't realize that the bridge is about to open for the ship.

"Uh-oh!" he says. "Boat too tall for bridge. What me going to do?"

Bizarro snaps his fingers. "Me know! Me rip big hole in bridge so boat can go through. Me smart hero!"

Bizarro lands on the roadway in the middle of the bridge. He reaches out and grabs one of the bridge's metal support cables.

RUMMMMMMBLE!

Bizarro turns his head and looks across the river toward downtown Metropolis. He sees a subway train traveling down the elevated tracks at the edge of the river. Bizarro has never seen a subway train before.

"Ooooh, look! Roller coaster!" Bizarro says. "Me love roller coasters!"

If Bizarro flies toward the subway train, turn to page 73.
If Bizarro chooses to stay on the bridge, turn to page 89.

"Bizarro, what are you planning to . . ." begins Superman.

"Me show you Bizarro's freeze-vision!" the creature says proudly. Then he soars over the platform in front of the Daily Planet Building.

"No! Don't!" Superman yells, as he flies in the air to stop Bizarro.

But the Man of Steel is too late.

A strong blast of arctic ice shoots out of Bizarro's eyes. Bizarro is facing the platform that is filled with dozens of people, including Superman's friends.

Soon, everyone on the platform is covered in ice. Each person is frozen in place. All of them have surprised looks on their faces.

"There," says Bizarro with satisfaction. "That cool them off!"

Turn the page.

"Me have another idea to cool off rest of city," Bizarro says to Superman. "Which way to dam in Metropolis?"

Superman's mouth falls open in surprise. The Mount Royal Dam is located several miles outside the city limits. The massive concrete dam provides water to both Metropolis and the farmlands outside the city. The dam also controls floods and supplies electrical power.

"Bizarro, you are *not* to go to the dam," Superman says sternly. "Do you understand me?"

"Yes, me not understand you," Bizarro agrees, as he flies away. "Me go to dam now."

Superman groans with dismay. He will have to chase after Bizarro. But first he has to deal with the frozen people on the platform.

Do I melt the ice by using my heat vision? he thinks to himself. *Or do I melt it by flying around the platform?*

If Superman uses his heat vision, turn to page 75.
If Superman flies around the platform, turn to page 92.

Bizarro releases Lois's hand and stands up. He heroically puts his hands on his hips and announces in a loud voice, "Me going to be hero. Me go to bank and help!"

Superman is curled up on the floor of the platform. He raises one hand and groans in pain.

"No . . . don't . . ." Superman says between clenched teeth.

Bizarro smiles at the Man of Steel and says, "My friend Superman agree it good idea. Me go now!"

"But me not know where to find bank," he says. "Me need better view."

WHOOOSH!

Bizarro zooms into the air.

High above the crowd, Bizarro spots the large Metropolis Savings and Loan building. "Me see it," he says. "Time to be hero."

Bizarro swoops to the bank and crashes through the front door. He quickly locates four burglars. They're standing outside a large steel vault and are trying to figure out how to open it.

BLAM! Bizarro crashes headfirst into the vault and tumbles to the floor.

"What are you?" asks one of the burglars with astonishment.

"Me am the hero Bizarro," he says proudly. "Me come to help!"

"Wait! We can explain," says one of the men nervously. "It's not what you think . . ."

"Me never try to think," Bizarro interrupts. "Thinking hurt Bizarro's brain. Me going to help open big door!"

CRRRRRRUNCH!

Bizarro reaches his arms wide and grabs the vault door. With a mighty tug, he yanks the steel door off its hinges. The four delighted men quickly run into the open vault.

"Me happy to help," Bizarro says cheerfully.

Turn to page 42.

The fire is now raging throughout the entire construction zone. Bright red flames fill the entire area.

Superman zooms into action and flies above one of the burning structures.

WHOOOOOSH!

The Man of Steel uses his freeze-breath to put out the flames in one building.

Bizarro is standing in the middle of the fire. He watches Superman with interest.

"Two heroes always better than one," Bizarro says. "Me help Superman with fire!"

The creature launches into the air and flies to a nearby park. He lands in front of a grove of elm trees.

"These trees what me need," says Bizarro.

Bizarro wraps his arms around one of the elm trees and squeezes with all his might.

CRUNCH!

The giant elm tree cracks in two. The top of the tree topples to the ground.

With a satisfied smile, Bizarro lifts the fallen tree. He flies back to the construction zone, carrying the tree in his arms. Superman is busy putting out the flames in another building.

"Me bring something to help," Bizarro says.

The creature raises his arms and tosses the elm tree into the middle of a burning building.

FROOOOOOOM!

The tree instantly ignites and sends a giant ball of fire high into the air.

"That how Bizarro help with fire!" he says proudly to Superman.

Turn to page 46.

Superman flies after Bizarro, but the strange creature is too fast. Bizarro flies a few feet above the street.

"Me use freeze-vision on street," he decides.

Bizarro opens his eyes extra-wide. Suddenly a steady stream of ice shoots out of his eyes.

Bizarro turns his head in all directions, blasting an arctic flow of ice through the air. Soon the entire street and sidewalks by the Daily Planet Building are coated with a thick layer of ice.

"There!" Bizarro says. "Me make winter wonderland!"

He turns to the crowd and says, "Now people can enjoy Superman party, thanks to Bizarro!"

The fire truck from the parade can't stop on the slick ice. It slides into a Superman Day float in front of it, crushing the back of the float.

CRUNCH!

Two people jump from the float seconds before the fire truck runs into it. They slip on the icy street and slide into the marching band.

OOF! OUCH!

A large man carrying a tuba falls over. His tuba flies through the air and lands on top of the dachshund dog.

YELP! YELP! YELP!

The dog runs into the street.

"Max! Come back!" yells the dog's owner.

The dog slides along the ice and runs into the Metropolis High School cheerleading team. One of the cheerleaders trips over the dog.

OUCH! OOF!

The cheerleaders topple like dominoes onto the ice-covered street.

Turn to page 49.

Back on the platform by the Daily Planet Building, the people watch nervously as Superman's breathing becomes slower and slower. Soon, he appears to stop breathing completely.

Jimmy Olsen climbs onto the platform and turns to Lois Lane.

"Miss Lane, we have to do something!" he says.

"Bizarro brought a box with him," Lois says to the crowd. "Where is it?"

Everyone on the platform quickly steps back and searches the floor below their feet.

"There's the box," yells Jimmy. "But it's empty!"

"Whatever was inside that box weakened Superman," says Lois. "We have to find it!"

Lois drops to her knees and begins to search. She sees the chunk of Kryptonite wedged into a crack in the platform. She quickly snatches the green rock.

"Quick, Jimmy," she says. "Put this rock back inside the box and close the lid."

After Jimmy completes his task, the people on the platform look anxiously at Superman. He's still not moving.

"Miss Lane, what are we . . ." begins Jimmy.

"Look!" says Lois. "His hand! Superman moved his fingers!"

With a gasp of pain, Superman stretches his fingers and then clenches them into a fist.

The Man of Steel groans as he slowly climbs to his feet.

"Thank you," he says, as he regains his strength and looks around the platform.

"Where is Bizarro?" he asks quickly.

"He said he was going to the Metropolis Savings and Loan Bank . . ." Perry White begins.

WHOOOOSH!

Before Perry can finish his sentence, Superman zooms into the air and flies away.

Turn the page.

Seconds later, Superman flies into the bank. He sees the giant steel door of the vault lying on the floor. Bizarro is standing next to it.

"Me solve bank problem!" Bizarro says proudly.

Superman shakes his head in dismay and quickly swoops into the vault. There he finds the four robbers filling bags with the bank's money.

"Sorry, boys," says Superman. "No withdrawals from the bank for you today!"

The Man of Steel flies toward the robbers and grabs their arms. He easily lifts the four men into the air.

Superman carries the four struggling men out of the bank. With a frown, he notices that Bizarro is gone.

After he drops off the men at the police station, the Man of Steel knows that he is going to have to deal with Bizarro.

"This is not how I wanted to spend Superman Day," he grumbles to himself.

THE END

To follow another path, turn to page 14.

"Me get more trees to help fire," Bizarro says, as he flies toward the park again.

Superman turns around to see what Bizarro has done. The flames are even higher now, thanks to the burning tree. The Man of Steel groans, knowing that Bizarro plans to help the fire by making it grow larger!

WHOOOSH! WHOOSH! WHOOSH!

Superman flies around the construction zone at super-speed, blasting each burning building with his freeze-breath.

Minutes later, the structures are still smoldering, but the fires are out.

Bizarro flies into view, carrying another giant elm tree in his arms. He looks disappointed.

"Superman put out fire," he says sadly. "How me going to help now?"

Bizarro lands next to Superman and drops the giant tree on the ground.

WHUMP!

"Should me burp again to make tree catch fire?" he suggests to Superman.

"No, Bizarro," says the Man of Steel. "No more fires."

Bizarro glances up at the blazing hot sun in the sky.

"It am very hot today," he says. "Me am going back to parade. Me help cool off people there!"

Superman realizes that Bizarro would use his freeze-vision to do this. He says, "No, Bizarro. I don't want you to freeze anyone in Metropolis!"

Bizarro nods his head and says, "Okay. Me do anything Superman tell Bizarro to do."

Superman pauses for a moment to think about Bizarro's offer.

"*Anything?*" asks Superman.

"Yes," agrees Bizarro.

Turn the page.

"Would you be willing to go somewhere else?" Superman asks. "Would you leave Metropolis for one year?"

"One year am long time for one hero in Metropolis," Bizarro says. "Am Superman sure he can do job alone?"

Superman smiles and says, "How about if we make a deal? If I need your help, I'll call for you."

Bizarro reaches out his chalky white hand to grasp Superman's hand. He energetically shakes the Man of Steel's entire arm.

"That am deal," the creature says. "Me see Superman in one year!"

ZOOOOOM!

Bizarro shoots into the air and flies away.

Superman shakes his head in disbelief and says, "All I had to do was ask. Can you believe it? *All I had to do was ask!*"

THE END

To follow another path, turn to page 14.

Bizarro is floating above the parade, watching the chaos below him.

"Now this what me call a *party*!" he says with a happy grin on his face.

"*That's enough!*" shouts Superman from the platform. The Man of Steel launches himself into the air and flies high above the icy street.

ZRRRRT! ZRRRRT!

Red-hot laser beams shoot out of Superman's eyes. The Man of Steel focuses his heat vision on the frozen street and sidewalks. He flies up and down the street. Soon, all of the ice is melted, and the people are standing in puddles of cool water.

"Water not as cold as ice," Bizarro says disapprovingly. "Bizarro make better choice than Superman."

Turn the page.

Superman flies up to where Bizarro is floating above the crowd.

"Bizarro, the last time you came here, we made a deal," says Superman. "You agreed to stay away from Metropolis for at least one year."

Bizarro nods his head in agreement and says, "Yes, but Bizarro no can tell time."

Superman sighs and wonders what to do next.

Bizarro looks down at the people standing in puddles of water in the street. The puddles are starting to heat up in the bright morning sunshine. The crowds are growing even more uncomfortable.

Bizarro looks up at the blazing hot sun and says, "Me have more ideas to help cool off people!"

Superman glances over at Bizarro and sees that the creature is looking at the sun. That gives the Man of Steel an idea.

"Bizarro, when you fly above Earth you can always see the sun, right?" asks Superman.

Bizarro thinks about this for a moment and says, "Yes, me can always see sun. Except when it night."

"That's right," agrees Superman. "And when the planet travels all the way around the sun, that's how you will know that a year has passed!"

"So me can know when it time to come back to Metropolis!" Bizarro says happily.

"Exactly," says Superman. "I think you've done enough for one day. Goodbye, Bizarro. I'll see you in one year."

"Me no have time to chat now," Bizarro says, soaring into the air. "Me have to follow Earth around sun!"

THE END

To follow another path, turn to page 14.

"Bank can wait!" Bizarro decides. "Me take Lois to our dream home now."

"What?" says Lois nervously. "We can't leave Superman here. He's hurt!"

Bizarro nods his head in agreement and says, "Yes, him must be hurt because you love Bizarro, not Superman. But love am strange."

Bizarro scoops Lois into his arms and flies high above the crowd of people. Soon Bizarro and Lois are flying high above the streets of Metropolis and heading toward the edge of the city.

"Put me down, *immediately*!" protests Lois. "Do you *hear* me?"

"Me have super-hearing," Bizarro replies. "Me can hear you shout very well."

Lois sighs with frustration. Then her nose begins to sniff.

"What *is* that smell?" she asks.

"That our new home!" Bizarro says proudly.

Lois' eyes widen as she sees where Bizarro is taking her. They have arrived at the Metropolis City Dump at the outskirts of the city.

"This is where you're going to build a home?" she asks with astonishment.

"Me knew you would like it," Bizarro agrees.

He drops Lois on top of a grimy blue sofa. It's stained with food spills. A few broken sofa springs are sticking out of the cushions.

"Ow!" cries Lois, as she lands on a sharp, broken spring.

"You already choosing furniture for new home?" asks the creature. "Me knew you would be happy here with Bizarro!"

Bizarro puts his hands on his hips and looks around the dump.

"Now me build our dream home," he says.

Turn the page.

CRACK! SMASH! BLAM!

Bizarro zooms around the dump. He grabs a king-size mattress and tosses it into a clearing. He lifts the rusty body of a pickup truck and breaks it into two halves. He smashes two dining room tables together and gathers up the wooden pieces.

Moving with super-speed, he collects more and more trash from the dump. He uses the broken, soiled, and smelly objects to build a large structure in the middle of the dump.

When he finishes, Bizarro sighs with satisfaction and turns to Lois.

"Dream home done," he says. "Now you and me get married."

Lois stands up and walks over to Bizarro. She is no longer angry or frightened.

"Bizarro, you and I can't get married," she says. "And I can't live here with you."

The creature looks puzzled and asks, "Why not? You am not liking new home?"

"No, because I don't love you," Lois says gently.

Turn to page 62.

Bizarro smiles in agreement and says, "Superman right. This job not big enough for two heroes. Superman can deal with fire. Bizarro go help someone else!"

Superman hovers over the construction site and uses his freeze-breath to cover the flames with ice. While he does that, Bizarro flies away.

Soon the creature is soaring high above downtown Metropolis. In the distance he can see the large metal globe on top of the Daily Planet Building.

"That look like world me protecting," Bizarro says, as he flies closer to the globe. "But me wonder why it not spin like real world."

Bizarro lands on top of the Daily Planet Building. He reaches out his hand and smacks the giant globe three times.

KLONK! KLONK! KLONK!

"This world not spinning," he says. "Me fix."

Bizarro wraps both of his arms around the globe.

SQUEEEEEEAK!

The steel braces at the bottom of the globe start to squeal as Bizarro tries to twist the giant metallic structure.

"World is stuck," Bizarro says. "Me need to push harder."

As Bizarro strains to turn the globe, the steel rods that anchor the structure start to twist and wobble dangerously.

CRACK! CRACK!

The rods at the bottom of the globe break in half. The giant globe begins to rotate.

"Now this look more like real world!" Bizarro says as he spins the globe faster and faster.

SCREEEEEECH!

Sparks fly in the air as the globe spins so fast that it becomes a blur. Seconds later, the giant globe topples over with a crash. With a loud rumble, the globe rolls across the rooftop and heads right toward the edge.

Turn the page.

"*Eeek*! Look up there!"

People are screaming on the street below as the giant globe teeters on the edge of the rooftop.

Bizarro is standing a few feet away from the globe. He looks puzzled.

"Me no understand why world stop moving," he says. "Maybe world need another push."

TAP!

Bizarro reaches out and touches the giant globe with one finger. It tilts off the side of the building and plummets toward the frightened people below.

WHOOOOSH!

Superman zooms into view.

The Man of Steel quickly swoops beneath the falling globe and stretches out his arms.

BLAM!

The Man of Steel stops the shattered globe from falling any farther.

Turn to page 65.

Superman reaches out to grab Bizarro, but the creature pulls away. Bizarro soars into the air.

"Fire hydrants filled with cold water," Bizarro says as he flies high above the crowd. "So me let water out to cool people off."

Bizarro lands on the sidewalk in front of a bright red fire hydrant. He stares at it for a few moments.

"Me not know how to open it," he admits. "So me will break it open."

Bizarro leans down and grabs hold of the top of the hydrant.

CRUNCH!

Using his super-strong hands, the creature rips off the top of the hydrant. A gushing stream of water shoots out. The water slams into a man standing nearby, knocking him to the ground.

"No need to thank Bizarro," the creature says to the fallen man. "You welcome."

Turn the page.

Bizarro works his way up and down the street. Each time he comes to a fire hydrant, he rips off its top.

Soon dozens of fire hydrants are spouting water into the air. The people in the parade scream and run for cover, desperately trying to escape the flowing water. They start slipping and falling on the wet street.

People and animals crash into the parade floats. Several floats smash into nearby buildings.

The Metropolis fire chief watches the chaos from the platform in front of the Daily Planet Building. He has a worried look on his face as he turns to the Man of Steel.

"Superman, you have to stop this creature!" the fire chief says. "We need that water to fight fires in Metropolis!"

"I'm on it, Chief," says Superman, as he launches into the air.

Superman flies over the flooded street. In the distance he can see Bizarro breaking open more fire hydrants.

"Superman, help! Help me!"

The Man of Steel hovers in midair. A little girl with blonde hair is calling out to him. He flies over to the girl and crouches down to face her.

"What is it? What's wrong?" asks Superman.

"It's Duke, my kitty-cat," she says between sobs. "He ran away and now I can't find him!"

Superman stands up and looks around. Water is streaming out of fire hydrants. People are running and slipping everywhere he looks. Superman focuses on a nearby mailbox. He uses his X-ray vision to peer at the metal structure.

Under the mailbox is a wet and frightened brown and white cat.

Turn to page 67.

Back at the Daily Planet, Jimmy Olsen climbs the steps up to the platform. Superman is sprawled on the floor and is groaning softly.

"Something in that box must have weakened Superman," Jimmy says, grabbing the empty box.

Thinking fast, Jimmy drops to his knees and searches the platform. He finds the small green rock wedged within a crack.

"Maybe this is what hurt Superman," says Jimmy, placing the green rock inside the lead box. He then tosses it far away from the platform.

Seconds later, the Man of Steel is feeling better. He stands up and looks around.

"Where is Bizarro?" asks Superman. "And Lois?"

Perry White points toward the east and says, "Bizarro took Lois. They went that way."

ZOOOOOM!

A few minutes later, Superman arrives at the city dump.

Lois Lane is standing next to Bizarro. A tear trickles down his craggy white face.

"Lois Lane no love Bizarro," the creature says between sobs. "Me not know what to do."

Superman places his hand on Bizarro's shoulder. Although Bizarro often causes a lot of trouble, the Man of Steel feels sorry for him.

"Bizarro, I have a plan," says Superman.

"You help Lois learn to love Bizarro?" the creature asks.

Superman shakes his head and says with kindness, "No, but I think I know a place where you'll be happy."

"Bizarro go with Superman to be hero?" the creature asks hopefully.

Superman soars into the air and says, "That's right. Follow me."

"Goodbye, Bizarro," says Lois. "Thank you for building this home."

"You welcome," says Bizarro, as he flies alongside Superman. "Me hope you very happy living here, Lois."

Turn the page.

Soon, Superman and Bizarro are flying deep into outer space. Far from Earth, Superman has located one of the most amazing worlds in the cosmos. It's a square planet!

Everything on this cube-shaped world is backward or wrong. City skyscrapers lean crookedly at all angles. The streets are filled with giant potholes. The bridges that stretch across the rivers have giant gaps in the middle.

As Superman and Bizarro fly closer, they see that the people on the planet all look like Bizarro. The people use coal instead of money. They proudly crash their cars into buildings. The sanitation workers throw trash from their trucks. Every street has an ugliness parlor.

"Goodbye, Superman," says Bizarro as he flies toward his new home. "Me going to be very happy here!"

THE END

To follow another path, turn to page 14.

Bizarro peers over the edge of the roof and watches Superman place the globe safely on the ground.

"My work done here," Bizarro says. "Me know just where to go now!"

The creature zooms into the air and flies toward the edge of the city. Soon he arrives at the Metropolis City Dump.

SQUISH!

Bizarro lands on a pile of large plastic bags. Each bag is stuffed with trash. The smell of rotting food fills the air. A few large gray rats scuttle out from holes in the bags and look up at Bizarro.

The creature thrusts his hand into a plastic bag and pulls out the remains of a fish. Bizarro tosses the sharp bones into his mouth.

"*Yum!* Someone left best part of fish!" he says, munching on the bones.

Bizarro reaches out to pick up one of the rats. He places the rat on his shoulder.

Turn the page.

"Me name you Rat," Bizarro says.

A few minutes later, Superman arrives at the dump. He finds Bizarro stacking a large pile of car tires. All of the tires are filled with holes.

"Hello, Superman," says Bizarro. "Me find lots of treasure here. Holes in tires make them very valuable!"

"Does that mean you're going to collect more of these instead of being a hero?" Superman asks.

"Yes, me sorry to disappoint you," Bizarro replies. "But me no have time to find more treasures *and* be hero!"

"But no worry, Superman," Bizarro says, scooping up the tattered tires in his arms. "Me come back when Superman need me!"

As Bizarro flies away, Superman sighs with relief. It's going to be a very long time before the Man of Steel needs help from Bizarro.

THE END

To follow another path, turn to page 14.

Superman walks over to the mailbox. He reaches down and uses his super-strength to easily lift and move the large metal box. The frightened cat jumps up into his arms.

"You're going to be okay, Duke," Superman says soothingly, as he returns the cat to the little girl.

"Now to deal with Bizarro!" says Superman.

Zooming into action, Superman soars down the street. As he flies over the open fire hydrants, he zaps each hydrant with his heat vision. The laser-like rays melt the top of each hydrant. The molten metal quickly forms a new cap that stops the flow of water.

Bizarro flies over to one of the fire hydrants that Superman has repaired. The creature looks puzzled by Superman's actions.

"Superman stop water," he says to the Man of Steel. "Superman have better idea?"

Turn the page.

Superman turns to face Bizarro. He puts his hand on the shoulder of the confused creature.

"Bizarro, I know you meant well . . ." begins Superman.

Bizarro interrupts Superman and says, "Yes, me great hero like Superman. In fact, Bizarro make great teammate for Superman. Me much better partner than Batman!"

Superman tries to hide a smile as he continues to talk to Bizarro.

"You see, Bizarro," says Superman. "That's the problem. I don't think Metropolis needs two heroes with all the powers we have."

Bizarro frowns as he thinks about this.

"You mean Bizarro and Superman in one place too much power?" he asks.

Superman nods his head and says, "Something like that."

"Me understand," Bizarro says. "From now on, me come to Metropolis only when Superman call for Bizarro."

"That's fine," agrees Superman.

"Me go to Gotham City instead. See if Batman need Bizarro's help," the creature says as he launches into the air.

Superman watches Bizarro fly away.

I'd better give Bruce Wayne a call and warn him, thinks Superman.

THE END

To follow another path, turn to page 14.

"If Bizarro leave with Superman, where we go?" the creature asks.

"We're going someplace I think you will like," says the Man of Steel. The creature smiles and takes Superman's hand.

Soon, Superman and Bizarro fly up and leave Earth's atmosphere. They zoom through the solar system, past Mars, Jupiter, Saturn, and Pluto.

"We there yet?" asks Bizarro.

"Not yet," replies Superman.

An hour later, they are soaring past hundreds of planets in the Milky Way galaxy.

For the eighty-second time, Bizarro asks, "We there yet?"

"Almost there," says Superman.

Suddenly, Superman stops and points toward a planet in the distance. Bizarro gasps as he beholds one of the strangest planets in the universe. It is a square world! Continents and oceans fill all six sides of the cube-shaped planet.

Turn to page 72.

"That a beautiful world," Bizarro says happily.

"I thought you would like it," says Superman. "But the best is yet to come."

Bizarro turns to Superman and asks eagerly, "You and Bizarro are going to live on this world and team up to be heroes forever?"

Superman quickly changes the subject and says, "Let's go down and explore the planet."

"Me right behind you," says Bizarro, as they enter the planet's atmosphere.

Turn to page 77.

Bizarro forgets all about the bridge and the ship.

Instead, he flies across the river and heads straight toward the subway train speeding along the elevated railway. He thinks the subway train is a roller coaster!

Bizarro lands on top of the moving train. As the train travels down the track, Bizarro sits on top of a subway car. His red cape flutters in the wind behind him.

"Faster! Faster!" he calls out.

After a few minutes, he frowns and says, "This roller coaster not going fast enough! Me not having fun!"

Bizarro stands up and peers at the track ahead of the train.

"Me know how to make ride more fun," he says to himself.

Turn the page.

Bizarro leaps into the air and flies in front of the subway train. Soon, he is almost a mile ahead of the train.

He lands in the middle of the elevated railway and smiles.

"Me use Bizarro-strength to rip out roller coaster tracks," he says a laugh. "Roller coaster then have to jump over hole. That make ride much more fun!"

CRUNCH! BLAM! CRUNCH!

Bizarro's muscles strain as he smashes the metal rail on one side of the tracks. He then breaks the rail on the other side. After that, Bizarro stomps his feet and knocks the wooden beams loose with his feet. The beams fall to the ground far below and splinter into pieces.

After ripping a gaping hole in the elevated railway, Bizarro looks pleased with his work.

Turn to page 79.

Superman faces the platform and narrows his eyes. A thin, laser-hot ray shoots out of his eyes. He is careful not to use the full power of his mighty heat vision. He slowly melts the ice around the people on the platform.

A few minutes later, the ice has melted, and the people on the platform are able to move.

"Superman!" calls out Lois Lane. "You saved us. Where is —"

"Sorry Lois, I have to go."

Before Lois can respond, Superman zooms away. He flies quickly to the Mount Royal Dam outside the city.

When he arrives, he sees that Bizarro is standing at the top of the dam. The creature is pounding his mighty fists against the concrete dam. Water is flowing over the top and creating a deafening roar below.

Bizarro looks up and waves to Superman.

"Me open dam so water can go to Metropolis and cool people off," the creature explains.

Turn the page.

Bizarro pulls back his arm and punches the concrete dam with all his might.

CRACK!

A giant hole appears at the top of the dam. A jet of water shoots through the hole and knocks Bizarro off his feet.

Bizarro tumbles down the side of the massive dam. He bumps his head over and over against the concrete.

BLAM! BLAM! BLAM!

"Ouch! Ouch! Ouch!" Bizarro yells.

Superman swoops down and grabs Bizarro's cape. He carries the grateful creature over to a grassy bank at the side of the dam and drops him there.

Superman looks over at the dam. The hole has grown larger, and more water is gushing through it.

Turn to page 82.

After they land on the square planet, Bizarro is delighted to see that all the people there look just like him. The men, women, children — even the animals — all have chalky, craggy white skin.

Bizarro decides to explore. He flies over a zoo where animals are roaming free and the people are in cages. Children are buying bowls of steaming hot melted cream from carts.

Bizarro visits a couple in one house. The woman proudly points out that they have put their rug on the ceiling.

"It never wear out," she says.

"And wallpaper on floor am very practical," says the man.

Bizarro returns to Superman and says, "Me sorry to disappoint Superman, but me can no longer be hero on Earth. Me am staying here."

Superman moves his hand to his mouth to cover a smile. He says, "I'll miss you, Bizarro. But I think you're making the right decision."

THE END

To follow another path, turn to page 14.

Bizarro flies back to the subway train and lands on one of the cars.

"Me hope roller coaster passengers appreciate the hard work that Bizarro doing," he says. "It not easy being hero!"

TOOOOOOOOT!

The train's engineer anxiously blows the train's whistle. The train is rapidly approaching the gaping hole in the middle of the tracks.

A few passengers look out the train's windows. They start to scream.

"Oh, good," says Bizarro. "Passengers having fun now!"

The train engineer frantically pulls on the brake lever, but it's too late. The train is just a few hundred feet from the hole in the tracks. Soon, the train will go hurtling through the hole in the elevated railway.

Turn the page.

WHOOSH!

Superman soars into view and flies alongside the subway train.

Bizarro waves at the Man of Steel. He happily calls out, "Superman want to ride roller coaster with Bizarro?"

Superman zooms ahead of the quickly moving subway train and dives in front of it.

The Man of Steel thinks fast and lands on top of the gaping hole in the middle of the railway tracks. He reaches out his arms and legs. He strains his muscles to stretch his body as far as possible.

Superman grabs one edge of the hole in the broken tracks with his hands. He props his feet over the other edge of the hole.

The train is inches away from the Man of Steel's outstretched body!

RUMMMMBLE!

The subway train rolls safely over the Man of Steel's back. The train once again connects with the tracks on the other side and travels down the elevated railway. The passengers are saved!

The Man of Steel quickly swoops down to the ground to grab the broken pieces of track. When he returns, he uses his heat vision to fuse the broken parts back together.

Bizarro appears and lands on the tracks next to Superman. "Me see that everything good here," calls out Bizarro, as he flies away. "Me keep working to help Metropolis!"

Superman continues to repair the hole in the railway. He sighs quietly to himself.

Superman knows that it's going to be a long day cleaning up after Bizarro's heroic actions.

THE END

To follow another path, turn to page 14.

CRACK!

The hole widens in the dam, sending chunks of concrete flying through the air. A mighty river of water surges through the hole. The water floods onto the land and flows toward Metropolis.

"The pressure of the water is going to make that hole in the dam even bigger," Superman says. "If I don't act fast, the dam will burst, and Metropolis will be flooded."

Superman looks around and makes a quick decision.

WHOOOSH!

He zooms through the air with both of his arms extended. He flies toward a giant boulder perched on top of a mountain at the edge of the dam.

BLAM!

Superman's fists collide with the giant boulder. The impact knocks the boulder loose, and it starts to roll down the mountain. Superman swoops around in front of the rolling boulder. He plants his feet on the ground and faces the giant boulder as it barrels toward him. He reaches forward.

WHAM!

Using all his strength, Superman stops the massive boulder. The Man of Steel breathes a quick sigh of relief. Then, lifting the huge boulder, he leaps into the air and carries it toward the top of the dam.

Bizarro is standing on the grassy bank on the other side of the dam. He watches Superman with puzzlement.

"Why Superman playing with rolling stone?" he wonders out loud.

Turn to page 85.

WHOMP!

Superman wedges the giant boulder into the hole that Bizarro created at the top of the dam.

The flowing water soon decreases to just a slight trickle.

Bizarro flies over to Superman. The creature looks annoyed.

"Me very angry," he says. "If Superman no want Bizarro's help, me no stay here!"

Superman can't believe his good luck. Is it really that easy to get rid of Bizarro?

"Metropolis not big enough for two heroes," Bizarro calls out, as he zooms into the air. "Good luck being only hero!"

"This really has been the best Superman Day ever," Superman says with a smile.

THE END

To follow another path, turn to page 14.

"Me sorry," Bizarro say stubbornly, "but me no want to go!"

The creature then lets out a loud burp, causing a blast of hot flames to shoot from his mouth. A wooden railing on one side of the platform catches on fire. Superman quickly flies over and uses his freeze-breath to douse the fire.

Losing his patience, Superman grabs Bizarro's wrist and pulls the creature into the air.

"You're coming with me!" insists Superman.

ZOOOOOM!

Bizarro smiles as Superman pulls him high above the Daily Planet Building.

"Oh, boy!" says the creature. "Superman going to team up with Bizarro. Me show you how Bizarro be big hero!"

The creature pulls his hand free and zooms toward a nearby building.

Oh no, thinks Superman. *What is Bizarro going to do now?*

Bizarro flies toward a tall apartment building. He waves to a man who is leaning out a window and staring as Bizarro heads directly toward him.

"That man about to fall. Me show Superman how me can save him," Bizarro says.

KER-BLAM!

The creature misses the man and slams into the wall of the building. The impact causes the man to fall from his window. It also loosens a dozen bricks in the wall. Both the man and the bricks go tumbling down the side of the building.

"Help! Help! Help me!" yells the man.

Bizarro zooms toward the screaming man.

"Look, Superman!" calls out Bizarro. "Me can use super-speed to save falling man."

ZAAAAAAP! ZAAAAAAP!

Superman flies into action and uses his heat vision to blast the falling bricks before they can land on the ground. The bricks explode into harmless dust.

Turn the page.

Meanwhile, Bizarro catches the falling man and sets him on the ground. Then he zooms up in the air to talk to Superman.

"Me good hero too," the creature says proudly. "And me as strong as Superman."

"Bizarro, you are not . . ." begins Superman.

"Not as strong as Superman?" interrupts Bizarro. "Me prove it!"

Suddenly, the creature lunges for the Man of Steel. He throws Superman against the wall of a nearby building.

BLAM!

Superman smashes through the wall. He lands with a crash on top of a desk in the middle of an office. Luckily, the office is deserted.

Superman quickly stands up, only to see Bizarro flying through the hole in the wall. He is heading directly toward the Man of Steel!

"Now me show you how strong Bizarro *really* am!" the creature yells with pride.

Turn to page 96.

WOOOOOOT!

The ship's captain blows the horn again.

"No time for roller coaster now," Bizarro says sadly. "Me have to make room for boat!"

A car is headed straight toward Bizarro. A passenger in the car screams with fright. The car's driver frantically turns the steering wheel to avoid hitting the creature.

"No time to play bumper car now," Bizarro calls out. "Me going to make nice big hole in bridge for boat!"

Bizarro walks to the edge of the roadway and grabs one of the bridge's metal supports.

CRUNCH! CRUNCH! CRUNCH!

He rips the metal support in two. Then Bizarro moves down the bridge, destroying two more metal supports. A crack begins to form in the bridge's asphalt roadway.

Turn the page.

CRUNCH! CRUNCH! CRUNCH!

Bizarro rips apart the metal supports on the other side of the bridge. The walls of the bridge come loose, and the crack widens in the road.

Bizarro then jumps up in the air and lands with a thud on top of the roadway. A jagged hole opens in the middle of the road. Soon, the hole expands. It widens to form a gaping ten-foot-wide opening in the middle of the bridge.

Bizarro looks at the damage he's done. Then he looks at the approaching ship.

"Me need to make hole even bigger for boat," he says.

HONK! HONK!

Another car appears and is headed toward the gap in the middle of the bridge. The driver is frantically hitting his brake pedal, but the car skids along the roadway. Bizarro turns around to glare at the car.

"Hey, watch where you driving!" says Bizarro. "Me am working here!"

SCREEEEECH!

The car slides to a stop.

The driver leans out his window and sees that the front wheels of the car are dangling over the edge of the hole in the bridge.

"Help! Someone, please help me!" yells the car's driver.

Bizarro walks over to the car and smiles at the driver.

"You need hero?" Bizarro asks.

As he says this, Bizarro places one hand on the car. The weight of his hand tips the car even farther over the edge of the hole.

Turn to page 99.

"I have to stop Bizarro, but first I need to save these people," Superman says to himself.

He launches into the air.

ZOOM! ZOOM! ZOOM!

Superman flies in a circle around the frozen platform. He travels faster and faster. The swirling warm air quickly begins to melt the ice.

BLAM! BLAM!

The platform shakes violently as the melting ice cracks open. The shaking of the platform causes the lead box that Bizarro had brought with him to topple to the ground. When the box hits the ground, the lid is knocked open, exposing the shining green rock inside.

The people on the platform are shivering from being covered by ice, but they soon start to recover.

"Superman, you saved us!" says Jimmy Olsen.

Superman lands on the platform. Suddenly he starts to sway. A look of pain comes over his face, and he drops to his knees. The people on the platform watch with horror as Superman collapses in front of them.

"He's not moving," says the mayor.

Not far away is the open lead box. The box is hidden from view under the platform. Inside the box is a lump of green Kryptonite. It's the only substance that can weaken or even kill Superman!

"Miss Lane, we have to do something!" yells Jimmy Olsen.

Turn the page.

Lois reaches down to grab Superman's wrist.

"I can't feel a pulse," she says. "Something has weakened him."

Lois jumps to her feet and says, "It must be green Kryptonite. Everyone, look around. See if you can find it!"

The people on the platform drop to their knees and quickly search around the platform.

"I found it!" calls out Jimmy. "It's over here, Miss Lane."

Lois quickly runs to where Jimmy is pointing. She picks up the green Kryptonite and places it back inside the lead box. Then she comes back to check on Superman.

"He's breathing again!" she says with relief. "He's recovering!"

Superman groans softly as he slowly gets up on his elbows and knees.

"Bizarro . . . the dam . . ." he gasps.

Turn to page 103.

Bizarro comes crashing through the hole in the wall. He is about to collide with Superman!

WHOOOOOOSH!

Before Bizarro can reach Superman, the Man of Steel quickly inhales and blows a mighty blast of his super-breath.

The impact of the powerful gust knocks Bizarro backward. The creature somersaults through the air and tumbles back through the hole in the building. He drops out of view.

It's quiet for a few moments. Superman cautiously approaches the hole in the wall. He leans out to see if Bizarro is gone.

WHAM!

Bizarro shoots through the air like a skyrocket. Both of his arms are extended.

His hands wrap around Superman's throat, and he sends the Man of Steel staggering backward.

BLAM!

Bizarro and Superman crash through the back wall of the office.

Together they soar through downtown Metropolis. Bizarro's hand is clasped tightly around Superman's throat.

BLAM! CRASH! SMASH!

One skyscraper window after another is shattered into tiny shards of glass as the pair crash through a series of buildings.

ZAAAAP!

Superman shoots a blast of heat vision from his eyes, but his head is tilted too far back. The red-hot beam soars far above Bizarro's head.

Bizarro squeezes harder, tightening his grasp on Superman's throat.

The Man of Steel is having trouble breathing. He is choking and gasping for air.

Suddenly, Bizarro looks worried. He loosens his grip on Superman.

"Me no want to hurt you," the creature says.

Superman quickly recovers his strength and flies to a nearby rooftop. Bizarro follows him.

Turn the page.

"Bizarro, I don't want to hurt you either," says Superman. "But you can't stay in Metropolis."

Bizarro thinks about this for a moment. Then he nods his head in agreement.

"Me understand," he says. "Bizarro and Superman both too powerful for one city! Metropolis no need two heroes as strong as us. One hero is enough!"

Superman pauses to consider Bizarro's statement, and then he decides not to disagree.

"Me go away now. But if Superman ever need help, Bizarro always ready to be backup hero," offers Bizarro.

With a sigh of relief, Superman reaches out to shake Bizarro's hand.

"It's a deal," says Superman with a smile.

THE END

To follow another path, turn to page 14.

ZOOOOOM!

Superman arrives. He quickly flies above the bridge and then loops under it.

The Man of Steel reaches up and grabs the car as it teeters over the edge of the hole in the road. With a mighty burst of strength, Superman lifts the car high into the air and sets it safely on the bridge.

"Thank you, Superman!" calls out the driver.

The Man of Steel flies back to the middle of the bridge and looks at the giant hole that Bizarro created.

"Bizarro and Superman make good team," says the creature with a crooked smile. "You save car and me save boat!"

Turn the page.

Superman turns to face Bizarro. He frowns at the creature and says, "Bizarro, this is a drawbridge. Do you understand . . . *drawbridge*?"

Bizarro laughs and replies, "Draw bridge? Superman silly! Bizarro no am going to draw bridge! Bizarro no am artist! Bizarro am hero!"

With a chuckle, Bizarro launches into the air again.

"Superman can make bigger hole and save boat now," the creature says as he waves goodbye. "Me going to find more adventures in Metropolis to be hero."

Superman flies over to the side of the bridge and looks at the broken metal supports.

He holds the two ends of one broken support together and uses his heat vision on them. The metal heats up, fusing the two halves together. He moves up and down the bridge, joining all the broken metal supports.

Turn to page 102.

Superman then trains his heat vision on the broken hole in the road. The intense rays heat up and melt the asphalt and concrete on either side of the hole. Superman reaches down to press the hot material between his palms. He spreads the concrete until it covers the hole.

"This will hold for now," he says, "but to be on the safe side, I'd better close the bridge and move all the cars off it."

After Superman carries 18 cars off the bridge, he pauses for a moment to catch his breath.

This crisis has been handled. But where has Bizarro gone to now?

THE END

To follow another path, turn to page 14.

Superman is almost fully recovered.

"Hand me that box that Bizarro brought," he says to Lois.

"But, the Kryptonite . . ." Lois begins.

Superman takes the box from her and says, "It can't hurt me when it's inside a lead container. But I have an idea how I might use it to get rid of Bizarro!"

WHOOOSH!

Superman zooms into the air and soars high above Metropolis. He knows that Bizarro is about to cause trouble at the Mount Royal Dam.

Minutes later, the Man of Steel arrives at the dam. Bizarro is pounding his fists on the top of the concrete dam.

KLONK! KLONK!

Bizarro is trying to break open the dam to flood Metropolis with cold water and cool off the hot city.

Turn the page.

Superman flies high above the dam.

"Hey, Bizarro," he calls out. "Take a look at what I found!"

Superman is holding the lead box in his hand.

Bizarro looks up and says happily, "You found my present! You like it?"

"This is what I think of it," Superman says. He pulls back his arm and throws the box into the sky with all his strength.

Bizarro looks shocked and launches into the air to chase after the box.

"Why you do that?" he cries out. "Me go get box. Me bring back present for Superman!"

Superman smiles as he watches Bizarro chase after the box. The box containing the Kryptonite sails far, far away.

"Me sure Superman will like present," Bizarro says, as he zooms high above the Earth in chase of the flying box.

Soon, just as Superman planned, the friction from traveling through Earth's atmosphere burns up the box and its contents. After a few minutes, the box and the Kryptonite completely disappear!

"Me not coming back without present," Bizarro vows. He continues to fly into outer space, hunting for the box.

Back on Earth, Superman looks up at the sky.

"Bizarro is going to be gone a very long time searching for that box," says Superman with a sigh of relief. "Maybe forever."

THE END

To follow another path, turn to page 14.

AUTHOR

Steve Korté is a freelance writer. At DC Comics he edited more than 500 books. Among the titles he edited are *75 Years of DC Comics*, winner of the 2011 Eisner Award, and *Jack Cole and Plastic Man*, winner of the 2002 Harvey Award. He lives in New York City with his own super-cat, Duke.

ILLUSTRATOR

Darío Brizuela was born in Buenos Aires, Argentina, in 1977. He enjoys doing illustration work and character design for several companies, including DC Comics, Marvel Comics, Image Comics, IDW Publishing, Titan Publishing, Hasbro, Capstone Publishers, and Disney Publishing Worldwide. Darío's work can be found in a wide range of properties, including *Star Wars Tales*, *Ben 10*, *DC Super Friends*, *Justice League Unlimited*, *Batman: The Brave & The Bold*, *Transformers*, *Teenage Mutant Ninja Turtles*, *Batman 66*, *Wonder Woman 77*, *Teen Titans Go!*, *Scooby Doo! Team Up*, and *DC Super Hero Girls*.

GLOSSARY

brake (BRAYK)—a tool that slows down or stops a vehicle; people use brakes in vehicles such as bikes, cars, and trains

dachshund (DAHKS-hunt)—a breed of dog with a long body, brown or red hair, very short legs, and drooping ears

drawbridge (DRAW-brij)—a bridge that can be raised or moved to let boats pass underneath

engineer (en-juh-NEER)—someone trained to operate and maintain machines or vehicles such as trains

hydrant (HYE-druhnt)—a large, upright pipe with a valve connected to a water supply for use against fires and in other emergencies

ignite (ig-NITE)—to set fire to something

lead (LED)—a soft, gray metal

subway (SUHB-way)—a system of trains that often runs underground in a city

vault (VAWLT)—a strong, secure room used to store money or valuables

BIZARRO

Real Name:
unknown

Occupation:
Super-Villain

Base:
Bizarro World

Height:
6 feet 3 inches

Weight:
235 pounds

Eyes:
Yellow

Hair:
Black

Bizarro is a botched clone of Superman created by Lex Luthor. While Bizarro has the strength and speed of the Man of Steel, he is unpredictable and doesn't realize his own strength. While he tries to be like Superman, he never quite gets it right and ends up causing trouble instead. He often has good intentions, but he doesn't grasp the difference between right and wrong. He doesn't understand the negative outcomes of his actions, which makes him a dangerous threat to Metropolis.

- Bizarro's superpowers are exactly opposite from the Man of Steel. Instead of Superman's fiery heat vision, Bizarro blasts beams of ice from his eyes. And while Superman breathes powerful gusts of cold air, Bizarro burps deadly flames.

- Superman's greatest weaknesses also have the opposite effect on Bizarro. While Kryptonite can bring the Man of Steel to his knees, the radioactive rock makes Bizarro even stronger.

- Like the real Man of Steel, Bizarro feels a strong bond with *Daily Planet* reporter Lois Lane and wants to marry and protect her.

- Even mutated clones need a friendly pet. Bizarro once stole a pet from the Interplanetary Zoo in Superman's Fortress of Solitude. Like Bizarro, his pet, Krypto, was the opposite of normal. To show excitement and love, Krypto didn't wag its tail — it bit people instead!